S0-ASH-200

TREASURE ISLAND

Vol. 5: In the Enemy's Camp
Adapted from the novel by ROBERT LOUIS STEVENSON

THE STORY SO FAR:

Jim Hawkins relates his adventures as a boy during the quest for Treasure Island:

When seaman *Billy Bones* died at his family's "Admiral Benbow" inn on the English coast, a treasure map found in his sea-chest proved Billy had been in the crew of the late pirate, *Captain Flint*. With *Dr. Livesey*, *Squire Trelawney*, and *Captain Smollett*, they sailed on the schooner, Hispaniola.

But their crew included one-legged *Long John Silver* and others of Flint's old crew. Jim learned of their planned mutiny—and, ashore on Treasure Island, he encountered wild-looking *Ben Gunn*, one-time Flint crewman who had been marooned for three years. The pirates seized the schooner, but the treasure-hunters and their servants took over an abandoned stockade on the isle, which they held against attack.

Sneaking out of camp, Jim boarded the Hispaniola to find that one of its pirate guards, *Israel Hands*, had killed the other. He coerced Hands into helping him steer the schooner to a safe anchorage, but there the buccaneer tried to kill him. Pinned to the mast-head by Hands' knife, Jim fired one of his pistols... and Hands fell dead into the water....

Writer	Penciler	Inker	Colorist
Roy Thomas	Mario Gully	Pat Davidson	SotoColor's A. Crossley

Letterer	Cover	Production	Assistant Editor
Virtual Calligraphy's Joe Caramagna	Greg Hildebrandt	Irene Lee	Lauren Sankovitch

Associate Editor	Editor	Editor in Chief	Publisher
Nicole Boose	Ralph Macchio	Joe Quesada	Dan Buckley

VISIT US AT
www.abdopublishing.com

Reinforced library bound edition published in 2009 by Spotlight, a division of the ABDO Group, 8000 West 78th Street, Edina, Minnesota 55439. Spotlight produces high-quality reinforced library bound editions for schools and libraries. Published by agreement with Marvel Characters, Inc.

Copyright © 2009 Marvel Entertainment, Inc. and its subsidiaries. MARVEL, all related characters and the distinctive likenesses thereof: TM & © 2009 Marvel Entertainment, Inc. and its subsidiaries. Licensed by Marvel Characters B.V. www.marvel.com. All rights reserved.

Library of Congress Cataloging-in-Publication Data

Thomas, Roy, 1940-
  Treasure Island / adapted from the novel by Robert Louis Stevenson ; Roy Thomas, writer ; Mario Gully, penciler ; Pat Davidson, inker ; SotoColor's A. Crossley, colorist ; VC's Joe Caramagna, letterer. -- Reinforced library bound ed.
    v. cm.
  "Marvel."
  Contents: v. 1. Treasure Island -- v. 2. Treasure Island part 2 -- v. 3. Mutiny on the Hispaniola -- v. 4. Embassy--and attack -- v. 5. In the enemy's camp -- v. 6. Pirates' end?
  ISBN 9781599616018 (v. 1) -- ISBN 9781599616025 (v. 2) -- ISBN 9781599616032 (v. 3) -- ISBN 9781599616049 (v. 4) -- ISBN 9781599616056 (v. 5) -- ISBN 9781599616063 (v. 6)
  Summary: Retells, in comic book format, Robert Louis Stevenson's tale of an innkeeper's son who finds a treasure map that leads him to a pirate's fortune.
  [1. Stevenson, Robert Louis, 1850-1894. --Adaptations. 2. Graphic novels. 3. Buried treasure--Fiction. 4.Pirates--Fiction. 5. Adventure and adventurers--Fiction. 6. Caribbean Area--History--18th century--Fiction.] I. Stevenson, Robert Louis, 1850-1894. II. Gully, Mario. III. Davidson, Pat, 1965- IV. Crossley, Andrew.
V. Caramagna, Joe. VI. Title.
PZ7.7.T518 Tre 2009
[Fic]--dc22   2008035322

All Spotlight books have reinforced library bindings and are manufactured in the United States of America.

As the hot blood ran over my back and chest, I began to feel sick, faint...

...and terrified of falling into that still green water beside the body of Israel Hands.

Fortunately, his knife had come the nearest in the world to missing me altogether...

...and held me by a mere pinch of skin...

...so that my violent shudder tore it away.

I was my own master again...

...and I regained the deck.

After I had done what I could for my still-painful wound, I looked around me.

The ship was now, in a sense, mine.

I began to think of clearing it from its last passenger--the dead man O'Brien.

I should lie down in my own place, I thought with a silent chuckle...

...and enjoy their faces when they found me in the morning.

Hrrrrhhh...

The sleeper whose leg I struck groaned, but without awaking.

And then--

Pieces of eight! Pieces of eight! ⹂SQUAWWWK⹄

Silver's parrot-- Captain Flint!

Who goes?!

I tried to run, but--

Hoooph...

Recoiling, I ran full into the arms of a second man...

Bring a torch, Dick!

It was Silver's voice.

"Jim Hawkins, you're within half a plank of death...and, what's worse, torture. They're going to throw me off.

"But I says to myself, you stand by Hawkins, John, and Hawkins'll stand by you.

"You save your witness, and he'll save your neck!

You mean all's lost?

Ship's gone-- neck's gone!

"But I'll save your life from them fools and cowards-- so be as I can--if you save Long John from swingin'.

"What I can do, that I'll do.

"That's a bargain, by thunder! Understand me, Jim--I'm on the Squire's side now.

"How you done it, I don't know...but I know you've got that ship safe somewhere.

"And the doctor gave me Billy Bones' chart...

"I don't know why, but there's surely something under that, Jim--bad or good.

Will you taste, messmate?

No? Well, I'll take a drain myself. I need a caulker...

...for there's trouble on hand.

And this black spot-- 'tain't much good now, is it?

Jim, here's a curiosity for you.

DEPOSED

Soon after, with a drink all round, we lay down to sleep.

And the outside of Silver's vengeance was to put George Merry up for sentinel...

SNORRRR

...and threaten him with death if he should prove unfaithful.

SNORRR

It was long ere I could close an eye.

SNORRR

Silver slept peacefully, yet my heart was sore for him, wicked as he was.

Then... good-bye, Jim.

And about the treasure, Silver--

Look out for squalls when you find it!

Jim, I seen the Doctor wanting you to run for it--and I seen you say no, plain as hearing.

You and me must stick close, back to back, like...and we'll save our necks in spite o' fate and fortune.

Soon we were seated about the sand over biscuit and fried junk.

In wasteful spirit, they had cooked three times more than we could eat...

...and one of them, with an empty laugh, threw what was left into the fire.

I never saw men so careless of the morrow.

Sure enough, mates, they have the ship somewhere...

But once we hit the treasure, we'll find it.

Then we're off to sea like jolly companions!

Silver still had a foot in either camp, and there was no doubt he would prefer wealth and freedom with the pirates...

...to a bare escaping from hanging, which was the best he had to hope on our side.

Ay... but no one tree atop yonder plateau is that taller than any of its neighbors.

We'll have to settle it by the readin' o' the compass.

I think it's *that* one.

Are ye Blind Pew? It's clearly that'n over *there*!

Following Silver's reading, after quite a long passage...

...we landed at the mouth of the second river, running down a woody cleft of the Spy-glass.

Thence, bending to our left, we began to ascend the slope toward the plateau.

The party fanned out, shouting and leaping to and fro...

From time to time, I had to lend Silver a hand...

...or he must have fallen backward down the hill.

At length, the man upon the farthest left began to cry aloud... as if in terror...

He can't'a found the treasure.

Nay--for that's clean a-top!

NEXT:
PIRATES'
END?